Adapted by S. E. Heller

D1132588

SCHOLASTIC INC.
New York   Toronto   London   Auckland   Sydney
Mexico City   New Delhi   Hong Kong   Buenos Aires

If you purchased this book without a cover, you should be aware that this book is stolen property. It was reported as "unsold and destroyed" to the publisher, and neither the author nor the publisher has received any payment for this "stripped book."

No part of this publication may be reproduced in whole or in part, or stored in a retrieval system, or transmitted in any form or by any means, electronic, mechanical, photocopying, recording, or otherwise, without written permission of the publisher. For information regarding permission, write to Scholastic Inc., Attention: Permissions Department, 555 Broadway, New York, NY 10012.

ISBN 0-439-23401-8

© 1995-2001 Nintendo, CREATURES, GAME FREAK.
TM & ® are trademarks of Nintendo.
© 2001 Nintendo. All rights reserved.

Published by Scholastic Inc. All rights reserved.
SCHOLASTIC and associated logos are trademarks
and/or registered trademarks of Scholastic Inc.

Designed by Carisa Swenson

12 11 10   8 9/9 0 1 2/0

Printed in the U.S.A.

First Scholastic printing, September 2001

CHAPTER ONE

A New Town

"Wow!" said Ash. "Look at that!"

Ash and his friends Misty and Brock were walking down a street. All three were Pokémon trainers. They traveled to many places and had many adventures. Their Pokémon Pikachu and Togepi went with them.

Today the friends were passing through Palm Hills. There were many fancy homes. But one home was larger and fancier than all the rest.

"That mansion is huge!" cried Misty.

"Brr!" Togepi wished it could

live there! It looked great.

Just then, three men walked by the friends. The men were wearing suits. They looked up and down the streets.

"Did you find it?" asked one man.

"Not yet," said another.

"If we don't find it soon, the lady will be upset," the first man said.

"Pika pika," said Pikachu. It wondered what the men were looking for.

CHAPTER TWO

A New Pokémon

"Hey, it's a Growlithe!" said Ash. A Pokémon was kicking up dust. It looked like a large dog.

Growlithe seemed angry. As it jumped into the air, the friends could see something hanging onto its tail. A small pink Pokémon flew off. It looked like a little dog.

 It was
frowning.
"What's
that?" asked
Misty.

"It's a Snubbull," said Brock. "I
have never seen one before."

"Wow!" said Ash. He checked
his Pokedex, Dexter.

"Snubbull, the Fairy Pokémon," said Dexter. "Snubbull
frowns a lot, but it is kind."

"Look! Snubbull has pink rib-
bons on," said Misty.

Ash leaned over Snubbull. "So
you're a girl. Well, you must be a

grumpy girl like Misty. You sure were tough to chase that Growlithe around."

Misty and Snubbull both growled at Ash.

CHAPTER THREE

A Tight Hug

Now one of the men in suits spotted Snubbull.

"My lady, Snubbull has been found," he called.

A woman came running. Her name was Madame Muchmoney.

"I told you never to leave the house!" Madame Muchmoney

scolded. "I did not sleep a wink last night." She hugged Snubbull tight.

Snubbull squirmed and growled. She was not happy she had been found. But Madame Muchmoney did not let go.

The woman turned to Ash and

his friends. "Thank you so much for finding Snubbull. Would you care to join me for some tea?" She invited them to her mansion.

Pikachu and Togepi were excited. They were going to see what it was like to be rich.

"Wow!" said Ash. The group stood on a moving sidewalk. "It is really far from the gate to the door!"

Misty smiled dreamily. "It's like being in an amusement park!"

However, someone was not having fun. Snubbull struggled in

Madame Muchmoney's arms.

Brock looked
worried. "Something
is bothering Snubbull,"
he said.

CHAPTER FOUR

Snubbull's Perfect Life

Inside, the friends could not stop staring. The mansion was huge!

Madame Muchmoney scrubbed Snubbull's feet with a brush. "The outside world is dirty," said Madame Muchmoney. "Clean off well."

When the friends had wiped

their feet, Madame Muchmoney offered to take them on a tour. She showed them a beautiful bedroom. This amazing room was just for Snubbull's naps.

Even Snubbull's wardrobe was huge. Hundreds of outfits lined the closet. Madame Muchmoney was proud of Snubbull's clothes, but the Pokémon shook her head sadly.

Next they went to Snubbull's fitness room. Pikachu and Togepi had fun trying the exercise machines. Snubbull struggled to get out of Madame Muchmoney's arms, but the woman hugged her tight.

"With such a huge yard, wouldn't Snubbull be better off running outside?" asked Ash.

Madame Muchmoney did not think so. "The sun would be bad for Snubbull's skin," she said.

Madame Muchmoney took them to a large pool. It was Snubbull's own bath. Pikachu and Togepi splashed in the water. They had fun swim-

ming.

"With
such a perfect
life, Snubbull must
be very happy," said Misty.

Madame Muchmoney nodded.
"I will pay any price to make my
Snubbull happy."

Snubbull shook her head. She
kicked. She growled.

Brock had a feeling Snubbull
was not happy at all. "A perfect
life, huh? I am not so sure," he
whispered to Ash.

CHAPTER FIVE

Popcorn Balls for Snubbull

Now it was time for lunch.
Madame Muchmoney invited the
friends to join her. Pikachu had
never seen such a large dining
room. There were many dishes
filled with fine food.

"This is great!" said Ash.

"*Pika!*" Pikachu thought the

food was delicious, too.

"It really is good, right, Togepi?" said Misty.

"*Brr!*" Togepi liked it.

Only Snubbull would not eat.

"You do not like it, Snubbull?" asked Madame Muchmoney. "Chef! Take this back and make something Snubbull can eat."

The cook looked upset. "But I've used all the best foods for this," he said.

Madame Muchmoney was worried. "Snubbull has been eating less and less."

Just then, Brock had an idea. He looked in his bag. There he found some old popcorn balls. He gave them to Snubbull.

Happily, the little pink Pokémon ate the popcorn balls. She thought they were great! Everyone was surprised.

"From now on I will make you only the most high-class popcorn balls," Madame Muchmoney told Snubbull.

"Good job, Brock," said Ash.

"It was no big deal," Brock replied. "But I think Snubbull is unhappy with her life here."

"I think you might be right," said Misty.

CHAPTER SIX

Team Rocket Trouble

Outside, two teenagers were spying into the beautiful house. It was Team Rocket. Jessie, James, and their talking Pokémon, Meowth, were Ash's worst enemies.

"I want to live in a place like this," Meowth said dreamily.

"This place must be full of treasures," Jessie said.

Team Rocket decided to sneak onto the grounds. They wanted to see what they could steal. And they wanted to swim in Madame Muchmoney's pool.

Soon Meowth ran into Snubbull. The two Pokémon stared at each other. Then Snubbull licked

Meowth on the chin.

"Huh?" Meowth was surprised.

Just then, Snubbull saw Meowth's tail. It was curled like a lollipop.

"Hey you!" Some guards had spotted Team Rocket. Jessie, James, and Meowth started running away.

Suddenly, Meowth felt a pain coming from its tail. Snubbull was biting hard. It was hanging onto Meowth's tail!

"That hurts!" cried Meowth. "Get this thing off me!"

Jessie grabbed Meowth. She swung Meowth through the air. Snubbull tried to hold on but she went flying. The Fairy Pokémon landed in Madame Muchmoney's arms.

"What?" cried Madame Muchmoney. "My Snubbull got outside again?"

Now the guards were after Team Rocket. So were Ash, Misty, and Brock.

"Go, Weezing!" cried James. He threw a Poké Ball. A purple Pokémon rose like a cloud. It covered the yard with smoke. No one could see. Team Rocket escaped.

Snubbull tried to get out of Madame Muchmoney's arms. She wanted to chase Meowth, but soon it was too late. Team Rocket was gone.

"Thank goodness my Snubbull is safe!" cried Madame Muchmoney. "Do not leave the house again," she told Snubbull.

"Those guys will show up anywhere, anytime," said Misty, shaking her head.

CHAPTER SEVEN

An Arranged Marriage

That afternoon, Madame Muchmoney, Ash, Brock, and Misty were having tea.

"You know, Snubbull does not seem happy," Brock began.

Madame Muchmoney nodded. "She is nervous. Today she will meet her husband," she said. She

showed the friends a picture of
another Snubbull. He wore a top
hat and had a bone in his mouth.
His name was Winthrop
Snubbullfellar.

"I thought Snubbull must be
lonely," Madame Muchmoney said.
"That is why I found a husband for

her. Soon Snubbull will be married."

Snubbull kicked and shook her head as Madame Muchmoney carried her away. She did not want to meet Winthrop Snubbullfellar.

Ash, Misty, and Brock were shocked. "Do you think Snubbull is trying to run away because she does not want to get married?" asked Misty.

"Yes," said Brock. "And she is tired of being told what to do."

Ash nodded. "Snubbull does not seem free. What should we do?"

"We must help her," said Brock.

Meanwhile, Team Rocket was planning to steal Snubbull. They wanted to kidnap her for their Boss.

"We've got the perfect bait," declared Jessie. "What bait?" asked Meowth.

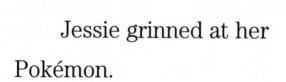

Jessie grinned at her Pokémon.

CHAPTER EIGHT

The Perfect Match

At the restaurant Snubbull was not happy. A well-dressed lady was talking to Madame Muchmoney. She was boasting about Winthrop Snubbullfellar's fancy life. Madame Muchmoney talked about Snubbull's fancy life.

"They are a perfect match," said

the rich lady.

"They sure are," said Madame Muchmoney.

Snubbull shook her head and kicked her legs. The other Pokémon chomped on his bone.

Suddenly, Brock, Ash, and Misty appeared. They had come to help Snubbull.

"Think about your Pokémon!" said Brock.

"We are," said Madame Muchmoney. "That is why we are arranging this marriage."

"But Snubbull is not happy,"

said Misty.

"I think your Pokémon would be better off living a more natural life," said Brock. Madame Muchmoney was confused. "But I do not let anything trouble my Snubbull," she said.

"Yes," said Ash, "and that is exactly the problem."

CHAPTER NINE

Meowth Bait

Just then, they heard someone
call out, "Ta-da!" It was Team
Rocket! They were standing on a
chandelier above Madame
Muchmoney's table. Jessie and
James lowered Meowth down to
the table on a fishing pole.

When Snubbull saw Meowth's

tail, she pushed her way out of
Madame Muchmoney's arms. She
grabbed Meowth's tail with her
teeth.

"We caught her!" cried Jessie
and James. They pulled Meowth
and Snubbull up.

"My Snubbull!" cried Madame Muchmoney.

"Give her back!" cried Misty.

"Do not worry. I know what to do," said Ash.

"Oh yeah?" said Jessie. She laughed. She and James threw down metal locks that wrapped around Ash's feet. They made Ash fall down. Misty and Brock fell, too. They were trapped!

Team Rocket escaped. And Snubbull was gone!

CHAPTER TEN

Trapped

Team Rocket was hiding in a shed near the restaurant. There were guards everywhere. Meowth had left Team Rocket's hot-air balloon at a park. Now they could not escape.

"This is your fault!" Jessie yelled at Meowth.

James began to shout at Meowth, too. Snubbull blocked him.

"Are you covering for me?" Meowth was touched. No one was ever nice to Meowth.

"I think that Snubbull actually likes Meowth," said Jessie.

Snubbull liked Meowth so much that she bit Meowth's tail again.

"Ouch!" screamed Meowth. It ran in circles. "Get her off me!"

Snubbull bounced around behind Meowth. It was fun.

"I am sure Snubbull's bite is just her way of saying she likes you," said James.

"I cannot take it anymore!" yelled Meowth. The talking Pokémon ran out of the shed, trying to get away from Snubbull.

CHAPTER ELEVEN

Battle for Snubbull

"Where could they be hiding?" asked Misty. She and Ash and Brock and their Pokémon were outside the restaurant, searching for Team Rocket and Snubbull. Just then, Meowth dashed out of the shed with Snubbull on its tail.

"There they are," cried Brock.

"Snubbull!" shouted Misty.

"This is bad," said Jessie and James. Jessie threw a Poké Ball. "Go, Arbok!" she yelled.

A giant Pokémon appeared. It looked like a snake.

"Go, Weezing!" cried James. Weezing used Smoke Screen. Black smoke filled the air.

Now Ash threw a Poké Ball.

"Go, Heracross!" yelled Ash. A Pokémon with a powerful horn appeared. It used Tackle on Weezing. Weezing crashed to the ground.

"Use Horn Attack on Arbok!" Ash called to Heracross.

Heracross tossed Arbok into the air with its horn. Arbok landed on top of Meowth and Snubbull.

"Ouch! That hurt," complained Meowth.

The little pink Pokémon crawled out from under Arbok. Then she bit the Snake Pokémon. Arbok hissed with pain. It was

chasing its own trainers!

"Stop it, Snubbull! You will get hurt," called Madame Muchmoney.

"Good work, Snubbull! Keep it up," called Brock.

"How dare you?" Madame Muchmoney said to Brock. She did not like someone else telling her Pokémon what to do.

"Just watch. Snubbull wants to use Tackle on Arbok," Brock replied.

Snubbull built up her energy. She crashed into Arbok. This was

great fun!

"Arbok! Use Tackle, too!" cried Jessie.

Arbok flew at Snubbull. Its strong body knocked Snubbull to the ground.

"Oh, no!" cried Madame Muchmoney. Still, Snubbull did not give up.

Snubbull rose into the air. She used Scary Face Attack.

Arbok was scared! Jessie and James screamed. Then Snubbull grabbed Arbok with her teeth. It was a great bite!

"Pika pika!" cried Pikachu. Snubbull was having a great battle.

Now James threw a Poké Ball. "Go, Victreebel!" he called.

A Plant Pokémon appeared. Snubbull jumped on Victreebel. Snubbull bounced up and down. She was having fun!

Suddenly, Team Rocket's hot-air balloon floated nearby.

"Just in time! Run for it!" cried
Jessie.

Team Rocket jumped into the
balloon. It started to float away.

Snubbull stared after the balloon. She did not want Meowth to
go.

"Heracross, use Horn Attack!"
called Ash. With its powerful
horn, Heracross sent Team
Rocket flying.

As the others cheered,
Snubbull stared at the sky. She
was still thinking about Meowth.

43

CHAPTER TWELVE

A New Beginning

"I learned my lesson watching Snubbull battle," Madame Muchmoney told Ash, Misty, and Brock. "I will let Snubbull lead a normal life. She needs more activity."

"That's great," said Brock. "Good for you, Snubbull."

"Pika!" Pikachu waved good-bye to Snubbull. It was time for the friends to be on their way. But Pikachu hoped Snubbull would be happy now that she could play outside.

Madame Muchmoney brought Snubbull to a fancy park. There were neat hedges all in a row. Madame Muchmoney let Snubbull play.

Snubbull looked around. It was better than Madame Muchmoney's house, but she was still not having fun. She started to imagine Meowth's tail. The more she thought about it,

45

the more she wanted to find Meowth.
With a burst of energy, Snubbull
ran right through the neat hedge. She
kept running. Finally, she was free!